PUFFIN BOOKS

MR MAJEIKA AND THE SCHOOL INSPECTOR

Humphrey Carpenter was born and educated in Oxford and worked for the BBC before becoming a full-time writer in 1975. He has published award-winning biographies of J. R. R. Tolkien, C. S. Lewis, W. H. Auden, Benjamin Britten, Spike Milligan and others, and is the co-author, with his wife, Mari Prichard, of *The Oxford Companion to Children's Literature*. From 1994 to 1996 he directed the Cheltenham Festival of Literature. He has written plays for radio and the theatre, including a dramatization of *Gulliver's Travels* (1995), and for many years ran a young people's drama group, the Mushy Pea Theatre Company. He has two daughters.

D1386092

Books by Humphrey Carpenter

MR MAJEIKA
MR MAJEIKA AND THE DINNER LADY
MR MAJEIKA AND THE GHOST TRAIN
MR MAJEIKA AND THE HAUNTED HOTEL
MR MAJEIKA AND THE LOST SPELL BOOK
MR MAJEIKA AND THE MUSIC TEACHER
MR MAJEIKA AND THE SCHOOL BOOK WEEK
MR MAJEIKA AND THE SCHOOL CARETAKER
MR MAJEIKA AND THE SCHOOL INSPECTOR
MR MAJEIKA AND THE SCHOOL PLAY
MR MAJEIKA AND THE SCHOOL TRIP
MR MAJEIKA JOINS THE CIRCUS
MR MAJEIKA ON THE INTERNET
MR MAJEIKA VANISHES

THE PUFFIN BOOK OF CLASSIC
CHILDREN'S STORIES (Ed.)

SHAKESPEARE WITHOUT THE BORING BITS
MORE SHAKESPEARE WITHOUT THE
BORING BITS

HUMPHREY CARPENTER

Mr Majeika and the School Inspector

Illustrated by Frank Rodgers

PUFFIN

PUFFIN BOOKS

Published by the Penguin Group
Penguin Books Ltd, 80 Strand, London WC2R 0RL, England
Penguin Group (USA) Inc., 375 Hudson Street, New York, New York 10014, USA
Penguin Group (Canada), 90 Eglinton Avenue East, Suite 700, Toronto, Ontario, Canada M4P 2Y3
(a division of Pearson Penguin Canada Inc.)
Penguin Ireland, 25 St Stephen's Green, Dublin 2, Ireland (a division of Penguin Books Ltd)
Penguin Group (Australia), 250 Camberwell Road, Camberwell, Victoria 3124, Australia
(a division of Pearson Australia Group Pty Ltd)
Penguin Books India Pvt Ltd, 11 Community Centre, Panchsheel Park, New Delhi – 110 017, India
Penguin Group (NZ), 67 Apollo Drive, Rosedale, North Shore 0632, New Zealand
(a division of Pearson New Zealand Ltd)
Penguin Books (South Africa) (Pty) Ltd, 24 Sturdee Avenue, Rosebank, Johannesburg 2196, South Africa

Penguin Books Ltd, Registered Offices: 80 Strand, London WC2R 0RL, England

puffinbooks.com

Published in Puffin Books 1993
Published simultaneously in hardback by Viking
This edition published 2010 for The Book People Ltd,
Hall Wood Avenue, Haydock, St Helens WA11 9UL
001 – 10 9 8 7 6 5 4 3 2 1

Text copyright © Humphrey Carpenter, 1993
Illustrations copyright © Frank Rodgers, 1993
All rights reserved

The moral right of the author and illustrator has been asserted

Set in Palatino

Printed in Great Britain by Clays Ltd, St Ives plc

British Library Cataloguing in Publication Data
A CIP catalogue record for this book is available from the British Library

ISBN: 978–0–141–33687–9

www.greenpenguin.co.uk

With thanks to the Wolvercote First School
for the idea of the lobster

Contents

1.   *It's not in the book*

It was a wet, dreary Monday morning at St Barty's School. 'Get out your maths books, everyone,' said Mr Majeika to Class Three. They all groaned. Having a teacher who'd once been a wizard could be fun sometimes, on days when Mr Majeika forgot he wasn't supposed to do magic any more, and spells and other odd things happened. But most of the time, nothing strange went on at all, and Mr Majeika just taught the usual boring lessons like every other teacher. Today looked like being that sort of day.

'How do you divide 36 by 7?' asked Mr Majeika. 'Does anybody know?'

Hamish Bigmore, the bad boy of Class Three, put up his hand. 'That's easy,' he sneered. 'You just use a calculator.' He took one out of his pocket and pressed the buttons. 'The answer is – '

'No, no, Hamish,' sighed Mr Majeika. 'You're not supposed to use a calculator. You're meant to . . . ' He froze, staring at something at the back of the classroom.

Everyone turned to see what it was. A face was peering in through the window: a long thin face, with a moustache that

was dripping wet, because the rain was pouring down hard. 'How odd,' said Mr Majeika. He went to the window and opened it. 'Can I help you?' he said to the man outside.

'Postlethwaite,' snapped the man. 'Inspector of Teachers. From the Government.' He had an official-looking briefcase under his arm.

'Oh?' said Mr Majeika. 'Well, nice to have met you, Mr Postlethwaite. If you don't mind, I must get on with my lesson. Goodbye.' He started to shut the window.

'Stop,' said Mr Postlethwaite, holding up his hand like a policeman directing traffic. 'Let me in. If door not handy, window will do.' He spoke in a very dry, clipped voice, as if he did not like wasting words.

'I'd rather you saw Mr Potter, the head

teacher, first,' said Mr Majeika.

But Mr Postlethwaite had already pushed the window fully open and climbed into the room. 'First part of Inspection of Teacher now finished,' he snapped. 'Time to begin second.'

'W-what was the first part?' stammered Mr Majeika, very flustered.

'Checking appearance of teacher,' said Mr Postlethwaite. 'Is he dressed tidily? Are his shoes polished? Is he wearing any unusual items of clothing.' He pushed his long thin face towards Mr Majeika, who stepped back in alarm. '*Have* you ever worn any unusual things?' he snapped.

'I-I used to wear a long pointed hat with peculiar signs on it,' answered Mr Majeika nervously. 'But that was when I was a wiz . . . I mean, before I became a teacher.'

Mr Postlethwaite opened his briefcase and took out a notebook and pencil. 'Used to wear a long pointed hat with peculiar signs,' he repeated, writing in the notebook. 'One penalty point.'

'What's a p-penalty p-point?' asked Mr Majeika anxiously.

'Penalty point is black mark. Get ten and you lose Teacher Licence. Not allowed to teach any more. Thrown out on street.'

'Thrown out on street?' echoed Mr Majeika, looking rather white.

Mr Postlethwaite took a large stopwatch from his briefcase. 'No more time-wasting! Ten minutes gone already. Only twenty left. Got to complete required amount of maths in time.' He started the stopwatch. It made a bleeping noise every ten seconds.

'Oh dear,' said Mr Majeika in a panic.

'But I've forgotten what we were doing.'

'You told us to divide 36 by 7,' said Thomas.

'And Hamish Bigmore wanted to do it with a calculator, but you wouldn't let him, Mr Majeika,' said Jody.

'I've done it without a calculator,' said Thomas's twin brother Pete. 'The answer is –'

'Shut up, cleversticks,' said Hamish Bigmore, sticking out his tongue at Pete. 'I bet you didn't really do it without a calculator. I bet you had one hidden under the table.'

'Hamish Bigmore, be quiet,' said Mr Majeika.

'Shan't,' said Hamish. He threw his maths exercise book at Pete.

'Hamish, if you don't behave yourself this instant,' said Mr Majeika, 'I'll – I'll –' He stopped. He could think of a lot of

things to do which would keep Hamish quiet, but none of them was likely to go down well with Mr Postlethwaite.

'Second part of Inspection of Teacher now beginning,' announced Mr Postlethwaite. 'Checking ability of teacher to keep order. How does his class behave? Are there any badly behaved girls or boys?'

'Do *they* get penalty points?' asked Mr Majeika hopefully.

'Not at all. Teacher gets penalty point for being unable to keep order. Or for using wrong methods to keep order. What are your methods?' he barked at Mr Majeika.

'My m-methods?' Mr Majeika scratched his head. 'Well, it's a little difficult to explain.'

'No it isn't,' shouted Hamish Bigmore. 'When he gets cross with me, he turns me into a frog.'

In fact this had only happened once, during Mr Majeika's first term at St Barty's School, but no one had ever forgotten it, and they were always expecting it to happen again.

Mr Postlethwaite opened his notebook once more. 'Keeps order by turning children into frogs,' he noted. 'Two penalty points.'

'Two?' gasped Mr Majeika. 'I only got one last time.'

'Use of magic by teacher strictly forbidden,' Mr Postlethwaite snapped. 'Not in Official Curriculum. Anything not in Official Curriculum carries two penalty points if used or taught by teacher.'

Mr Majeika looked stunned. 'Please, what's an Official – whatever you said?' he asked.

Mr Postlethwaite took a big black book out of his briefcase, and held it up for everyone to see. On the front, it said:

OFFICIAL CURRICULUM

What Is To Be Taught In Schools
As Decided By The People In Charge
Nothing Else May Be Taught
By Order

'No magic in Official Curriculum,' he repeated.

'Well, what is in it?' asked Jody.

'"What is in it, *sir*?"' said Mr Postlethwaite crossly. 'Pupils should address Inspector as "sir". Pupils should also address teacher as "sir", or, if female, "Miss". Teachers not being addressed as "sir" or "Miss" earn penalty point.'

'We never call *him* "sir",' laughed

18

Hamish Bigmore, pointing rudely at Mr Majeika. 'Nobody's ever called silly old Mr Majeika "sir".'

'Never been called "sir" by his pupils,' muttered Mr Postlethwaite, making another note. 'One more penalty point.'

Mr Majeika sat down, mopping his brow with his handkerchief. 'I can't take much more of this,' he said. 'Anyway, you never answered Jody's question. What *is* in the Official whatever-it's-called?'

'The Official Curriculum,' answered Mr Postlethwaite briskly, 'consists of itcms which the People in Charge have decided that schoolchildren must learn.'

'I suppose, *sir*,' said Pete to Mr Postlethwaite, 'that means things like the dates of the kings and queens of England?'

'And knowing your thirteen times

table, *sir*?' asked Jody.

Mr Postlethwaite nodded. 'Exactly. And much more like that. All very hard work. No shirking. No fun. No amusement. Work, work, work.'

'No school trips?' asked Thomas, forgetting to call Mr Postlethwaite 'sir'.

Mr Majeika jumped to his feet. 'Goodness,' he said, 'I'd quite forgotten. I'm taking you all on a trip to Barty Castle today. The bus must be waiting. Come along!'

Everyone cheered, packed up their things, and hurried out of the classroom, forgetting for the moment all about Mr Postlethwaite. Outside, the weather had cleared, and the sun was beginning to shine.

Mr Postlethwaite followed Mr Majeika across the playground to the bus, looking very cross. 'School trips firmly discouraged

by Official Curriculum,' he snapped.
'Penalty points for teachers who arrange
trips for fun.'

'Ah, but this isn't for fun,' said Mr
Majeika. 'It's a history lesson.'

Mr Postlethwaite took out his
stopwatch. 'Nearly forgot,' he said,
'Maths lesson not completed. One
penalty point.'

Mr Majeika sighed. 'How many have I

got left before you take away my Teacher Licence?' he asked.

'Five gone,' snapped Mr Postlethwaite. 'Five to go. At this rate,' he added with a nasty smile, 'it won't take you long to lose them.'

All the way to Barty Castle, Class Three sat gloomily in silence. They were glad to be going on a trip, but the sight of Mr Postlethwaite sitting stiffly next to Mr Majeika at the front of the bus made everyone depressed. Only Hamish Bigmore kept chattering away, in the hope of making Mr Majeika lose his temper and get into more trouble with Mr Postlethwaite.

He kept saying things like: 'Please, Mr Majeika, *sir*, can we have the window open, *sir*?' And then a moment later, after it had been opened: 'Please, Mr Majeika, *sir*, it's awfully cold now. Could we have the window shut again, please *sir*?'

'Do shut up, Hamish,' whispered Jody. 'If Mr Majeika loses his Teacher Licence, and isn't allowed to teach any more, we're bound to get someone really boring or horrid as our new class teacher.'

'There couldn't be anyone more boring or horrid than Mr Majeika,' sneered Hamish, but for the time being he shut up.

When the bus arrived at Barty Castle, the man who sold the tickets said: 'You may not want to go inside the Castle today. Something has gone wrong with the electricity, and there's no heating and no lighting.'

'Oh dear,' said Mr Majeika. 'Still, as we've come all this way, we'd better go in.' He led Class Three across the drawbridge into the castle, with Mr Postlethwaite following behind.

They went through a doorway into a dark room with a stone floor and roof. 'We'll start our visit here,' called Mr Majeika to everyone. 'Gather round and listen.'

'Brr, it's cold,' said Jody.

Mr Postlethwaite took a thermometer out of his briefcase. 'Temperature only

three degrees above freezing,' he said crossly, peering at it. Then he took out the Official Curriculum and read from it: 'Teachers shall ensure that all places where they teach are properly heated and lit.' He shut the Official Curriculum. 'This is not properly heated or lit. One more penalty point.'

'Oh dear,' said Mr Majeika. 'I don't seem to be able to do anything right. We must start our lesson. This castle was built in the time of Queen Elizabeth the First. Does anybody know when she came to the throne?'

There was silence. Class Three weren't good at remembering dates.

Mr Postlethwaite took out his notebook. 'Teacher has failed to teach dates to children. One penalty –'

He broke off, because Class Three had suddenly gasped aloud. Then, as one person, they all called out: '1558.'

What had happened was this. Behind Mr Majeika and Mr Postlethwaite was a dark passage. While Mr Postlethwaite had been making his note, the date '1558' had appeared out of nowhere, glowing in mid-air in the darkness.

'Correct,' called out Mr Majeika.

Mr Postlethwaite stopped writing in his notebook and looked cross. 'Teacher seems to have managed to teach *one* date,' he muttered.

'And do you know who came to the throne after her?' called out Mr Majeika.

Again, the answer appeared in glowing letters in the passage behind Mr Majeika and Mr Postlethwaite. 'James the First,' everyone called out.

'In which year?' asked Mr Majeika.

Once again, there was the answer, glowing in the dark. '1603,' they shouted.

Mr Postlethwaite seemed to suspect
some sort of trick, for he spun round and
looked behind him. But before he could
see them, the magical letters had
vanished.

'There you are,' said Mr Majeika
cheerily. 'They really do know their
dates. Shall we go further into the
castle?'

He led the way down the dark passage, and soon they emerged into a gallery which looked down into a big hall below. Mr Majeika stood with his back to the railing of the gallery, with Mr Postlethwaite alongside him. 'Now, everyone,' Mr Majeika called out, 'this is the Great Hall. Can anybody tell me what sort of things used to happen here in the old days, when the castle was first built?'

'They used to watch TV,' giggled Hamish Bigmore.

Mr Postlethwaite looked pleased. 'Just as I guessed. Teacher hasn't taught children anything about historical customs. One p –' But again he was interrupted, this time by a forest of hands going up.

'Yes, Jody?' said Mr Majeika, pointing at her.

'They had enormous banquets,' said Jody, 'which began with one of the servants carrying in a boar's head on a big gold dish.'

'And they didn't have knives and forks,' said Thomas. 'They used to eat with their fingers, and throw the bones to the dogs, who lay about on the straw which covered the floor.'

'And sometimes one of the knights challenged another one to a fight, and they had a duel with swords, usually over which of them was going to marry a fair lady,' said Pete.

'Well done,' said Mr Majeika.

'It was easy,' grinned Jody. And so it had been. Behind Mr Majeika and Mr Postlethwaite, in the Great Hall below the gallery, everything Jody, Thomas and Pete were describing had been happening, acted out silently by glowing

people whom Class Three supposed must be ghosts.

'Now,' said Mr Majeika, 'can anyone tell me what happened in this castle during the Civil War, in the seventeenth century?'

Again, there was a forest of hands, because everyone could clearly see the answer being acted out in front of them.

'Hamish, you tell us this time,' said Mr Majeika.

'Well,' said Hamish, with a wicked grin on his face, 'there was fighting between two lots of men. One group had long hair and looked silly, and the other had short hair, and looked even sillier.'

'What were they called?' asked Mr Majeika, and the answer flashed up over the men whom Class Three could see fighting each other in the Great Hall below: 'Roundheads and Cavaliers.'

'I don't know,' said Hamish, grinning even more, 'but don't you think they look silly, Mr Postlethwaite?' And Hamish pointed.

Mr Postlethwaite turned. But before Mr Majeika could make the soldiers vanish, Mr Postlethwaite had seen them. 'Thought so,' he said. 'Teacher cheating.

Using magic too. Four penalty points gone. That's it.' He turned to Mr Majeika. 'Your Teacher Licence is withdrawn, and you will not be permitted to teach again. No more job. Thrown out on street.'

'Oh dear,' said Mr Majeika miserably.

'It's not fair!' said Jody. 'He was only trying to help us.'

'Do not interfere,' Mr Postlethwaite snapped. 'Pupils who interfere will be removed from ordinary school and sent to institutions which will correct their behaviour. Now, lead us back to bus,' he said to Mr Majeika.

'Very well,' sighed Mr Majeika. 'Only, I think I may have lost the way.'

'It's just down there, Mr Majeika,' said Thomas, but Mr Majeika motioned to

him to be quiet. He led Mr Postlethwaite down a passage they hadn't come through before. Class Three followed behind.

'It's not far to the bus,' said Mr Majeika cheerily. But the passage got darker and darker, and soon they could not see where they were walking.

'Mistake has been made,' said Mr Postlethwaite, sounding rather nervous. 'Better turn round. Try other way.' And then he gave a shriek.

In front of him, barring the way down the passage, was an enormous glowing figure, a big fat man in a crown, holding an axe. 'It's Henry the Eighth!' whispered Jody. 'I recognize him from pictures in the history books.'

'Postlethwaite!' roared the ghost. 'Do you know who I am?'

'Y-yes, Your Majesty,' stammered Mr

Postlethwaite. 'You're the ghost of Henry
the Seventh. Er – I mean, Eighth.'

'You mustn't make mistakes like that,
Postlethwaite!' roared the ghost. 'You get
given penalty points for mistakes, and
when you reach ten, do you know what
happens? I chop off your head,
Postlethwaite! You've got one penalty
point already for your silly mistake,

Postlethwaite. Now tell me what were the dates of my birth and death, the date I came to the throne, and the names of my six wives. That makes nine questions, Postlethwaite, and you know what'll happen if you get all nine wrong, don't you?'

'Help!' gasped Mr Postlethwaite. 'Mind has gone blank. Can't remember a thing. Not a single date or name.'

'Can't you, Postlethwaite?' roared Henry the Eighth. 'Let's see if my axe helps you to remember!'

Mr Postlethwaite fell to his knees. 'No, no,' he cried. 'Spare me, and I'll spare Mr Majeika. I'll never inspect another teacher again, or take away his Teacher Licence. I'll run away and join a circus.'

'Better do just that, Postlethwaite,' roared Henry the Eighth. 'Because if you ever try to inspect another teacher

again, or bring out that silly Official
Curriculum, I'll be waiting for you!'
And with that, the ghost of the king
vanished.

So did Mr Postlethwaite. He took to
his heels and ran off down the passage.
When Class Three and Mr Majeika
came out into the open, they saw him

disappearing across the countryside.

'I hope he finds a circus,' said Jody. 'He's dropped the Official Curriculum on the grass.'

'Let's leave it there,' said Mr Majeika. 'Thank goodness, we won't be needing it.'

2. *A fishy business*

In the corner of Class Three's classroom
stood a large glass fish tank. It was full of
small fish of different colours, and there
were lots of water-plants, and gravel on
the bottom. It was in this tank that
Hamish Bigmore had swum about, when
Mr Majeika turned him into a frog.

Everyone in Class Three had to take turns cleaning out the tank, and feeding the fish. When it was Hamish Bigmore's turn, he never did it properly.

'Don't you like the fish, Hamish?' said Jody. 'Didn't you make friends with them when you were a frog?'

'Huh,' said Hamish crossly. 'The only fish I like is fish and chips.'

One morning, Mr Majeika told Class Three to bring their chairs and sit in a circle around the fish tank, so that they could have a lesson about underwater life.

'That's boring!' shouted Hamish Bigmore. He made a paper dart and threw it at Mr Majeika.

'Hamish,' said Mr Majeika, 'you'd better behave yourself, or else . . . '

'Or else what?' sneered Hamish. 'You wouldn't dare turn me into a frog again.

You wouldn't dare do *anything*.'

This was perfectly true. Whenever Mr Majeika lost his temper with Hamish and turned him into something, there was always a lot of trouble, and he wished he hadn't.

'I'll send you to Mr Potter,' Mr Majeika told Hamish crossly.

'Ha ha!' laughed Hamish. 'When you do that, silly old Mr Potter just sends me back again.'

This was true too. Mr Potter never seemed to know how to punish Hamish, except by sending him home, which of course was exactly what Hamish wanted.

'Let's get on with the lesson,' said Mr Majeika miserably, trying to pretend Hamish wasn't there. 'Who can tell me what sort of creatures live underwater, besides fish?'

A hand shot up. It was Hamish

Bigmore's. Mr Majeika ignored him, and turned to Thomas, who had put his hand up too. 'Yes, Thomas?' he said.

'Me!' shouted Hamish. 'My hand went up first. Ask me!'

'All right, Hamish,' said Mr Majeika wearily. 'What do we find living under the water besides fish?'

'Submarine crews. Ha ha ha ha!' laughed Hamish.

'Don't be silly, Hamish,' said Mr Majeika. Jody had put her hand up, so Mr Majeika turned to her. 'Yes, Jody?'

But Hamish wasn't to be stopped so easily. 'Submarine crews,' he said again. 'And the submarines have got lots of bombs on board, and they can come zooming up out of the water, and bomb everyone to smithereens, zoom, bam, zap!'

Melanie began to cry. 'Boo hoo! I'm

frightened of the submarines!'

'Hamish!' snapped Mr Majeika. 'Behave yourself!'

'You can't make me,' sang out Hamish. 'I'm going into the craft area to make a submarine. Get out of my way!' He barged his way past everyone and went through the door.

'Oh dear,' sighed Mr Majeika, 'I ought to go and fetch him. There's no one in the craft area to keep an eye on him.' The craft area was where Class Three did painting and woodwork.

'Leave him where he is, Mr Majeika,' said Pete. 'At least we'll have some peace to get on with the lesson.'

'I really shouldn't,' said Mr Majeika, but it was very nice to be without Hamish for a bit, so he went on teaching them about life under water.

The lesson had just begun to get interesting, with Mr Majeika telling them about some of the strange creatures that you find on the river and sea bed, when in from the craft area rushed Hamish Bigmore, holding an enormous piece of wood. 'Watch out, world!' he shouted. 'Here comes the Bigmore submarine, full of bombs!' He rushed straight for the fish tank, barging past everyone and overturning their chairs.

Probably he did not mean to do any

serious damage, but Thomas and Pete made a grab for him, and this was the cause of the disaster. Hamish tripped, the big piece of wood went flying, and hit the side of the fish tank with a smack. The glass cracked and burst open, and water, fish and gravel poured out on to the floor.

'Hamish!' shouted Mr Majeika, quivering with rage. 'I know I mustn't

turn you into anything, but – but –
but – ' And with that, Mr Majeika
vanished.

Thomas stared. 'What's happened to
him?' he gasped.

'I shouldn't worry,' said Jody. 'I'm
sure he can look after himself. We've got
to save all the fish and everything before
they die. Quick, there's an empty tank in
the science room – I'll fetch it, and Pete,
you go and get a bucket from the
caretaker and fill it with water and put
the fish in quickly.'

It took ages to sort everything out, but
at last it was all back to normal, with the
new tank on the table in place of the old,
and the fish swimming about in it,
looking a bit dazed but otherwise all
right.

'The only thing is,' said Pete,
'where's Mr Majeika?'

'What's that crawling about under the desks?' asked Thomas. 'It looks like we didn't put one of the water creatures back in the tank.'

Jody peered under the desks. 'Ugh, it's got claws,' she said. 'I think it's a lobster. I don't remember seeing it in the tank.'

'Nor do I,' said Pete. 'But we'd better put it in the water with the rest.' He fetched a broom, and they shooed it into the bucket, and then tipped it into the tank, where it began crawling about on the bottom.

Jody looked closely at it. 'Do you remember,' she asked Thomas and Pete, 'that when Hamish got turned into a frog, the frog looked rather like him? Come and see if this lobster reminds you of anyone.'

Thomas and Pete came and looked. 'Oh no!' gasped Thomas.

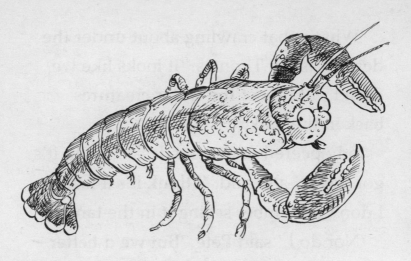

'It's Mr Majeika!' said Pete.

Sure enough, the lobster looked exactly like him. As they said his name, it came up to the glass and peered at them. 'I think it's nodding its head,' said Jody. 'It *is* him, it *is* Mr Majeika! What on earth has happened?'

'My guess,' said Pete, 'is that he was trying hard not to lose his temper and turn Hamish into something, but he couldn't stop himself doing a spell, and it was the wrong sort of spell, and now he's turned himself into a lobster.'

48

'So how is he going to turn himself back again?' asked Jody.

'He's not!' sneered a voice behind them. It was Hamish. 'Silly fathead Mr Majeika, he's really got himself in a fix this time. Good riddance to him! Yah! Silly old lobster!' And Hamish pushed his face against the glass of the tank and stuck out his tongue at the lobster.

49

'Oh dear,' sighed Thomas, 'I'm afraid Hamish may be right. How on earth is he going to get back to normal? Do you think lobsters can do spells?'

The lobster seemed to be shaking its head.

'I don't think they can,' said Jody. 'That means it's up to us.'

'Us?' asked Pete, puzzled.

'Well, someone's got to rescue him,' said Jody. 'We've got to try.'

The bell rang for the end of afternoon school, and everyone began to pack up their things and go home. 'I'll think about it at home,' Jody said to Thomas and Pete. 'You think about it too. I'm sure we can come up with a rescue plan.'

Next morning, Thomas and Pete came to school looking very gloomy. 'Haven't you got any ideas?' Jody asked them when she met them at the school gate.

They shook their heads. 'Not really,' said Thomas.

'We thought we could try and find Mr Majeika's spell book,' said Pete, 'and then say some of the spells, and maybe we'd find the right one.'

'But maybe we wouldn't,' said Thomas, 'and there might be awful trouble if we said the wrong spell.'

'And anyway,' said Pete, 'we don't know where his spell book is, and we're not wizards, so probably none of the spells would work for us anyway.'

'I'm sure they wouldn't,' said Jody. 'We need a real wizard to undo the spell – or a witch. Which is why I'm taking *this* to the post office this afternoon, to get them to put it in the window.'

She held out a card, on which she had written:

URGENT
Will the Witch known as
WILHELMINA WORLOCK
please contact Class Three,
St Barty's School,
AT ONCE!!!
Thank you.

'Wilhelmina Worlock?' gasped Thomas. 'You're not advertising for *her*?' Wilhelmina Worlock was a very nasty witch, who was always turning up at St Barty's in disguise and trying to take over the school.

'She hates Mr Majeika,' said Pete. 'Surely she wouldn't help us?'

'She wouldn't *want* to help us,' said Jody. 'But I've got a plan . . . '

The card was put up in the post office window that afternoon, and all the next day, Jody, Thomas and Pete waited to see if Miss Worlock would appear at St Barty's. Mr Potter, who had to teach Class Three because Mr Majeika had disappeared, got very cross with them for peering out of the window every time they heard a noise in the playground.

'It's not her,' sighed Jody, after yet

another false alarm. 'I'm afraid she's not coming.'

'Probably witches don't read advertisement cards in post office windows,' said Pete.

At that moment, the bell rang for the end of school. 'You can go home now,' called Mr Potter, and opened the door of Class Three. Then he jumped, because someone was standing right outside it: an old woman wrapped up in a big black coat.

'Hello, dearie,' she said in a voice that Jody, Thomas and Pete recognized at once. 'I'm little Jody's grandma, come to collect her. Mind out, will you?' And she elbowed her way rudely into the classroom, pushing Mr Potter to one side.

Mr Potter scratched his head. 'Haven't we met somewhere before?' he asked the

old lady. As she didn't answer, he
picked up his books and went off to his
office, still looking puzzled.

'Hello, Miss Worlock,' said Jody. 'You
remember Thomas and Pete, don't you?'

'Why, of course, my little dears,' said
Wilhelmina Worlock. 'And *you* remember
the Wilhelmina Worlock School of Music,
don't you, tee hee?'

Thomas and Pete nodded. They certainly remembered the dreadful time when Miss Worlock had formed a school orchestra, and had cast a spell which made them all get itchy fingers if they didn't practise their instruments.

'Would you like to do that again, Miss Worlock?' asked Jody. 'Have another school orchestra, and give a concert?'

Pete dug Jody in the ribs. 'You fool!' he whispered. 'We don't want her to do that. We want her to turn Mr Majeika back from a lobster.'

'Ssh,' whispered Jody. 'I know what I'm doing.'

'Why, yes, dearie, I'd love to,' said Miss Worlock. 'Especially if that silly weasly wizard Majeika doesn't interfere this time. Where is he?' she asked suspiciously, looking round.

'Oh, he's, er, gone for a seaside holiday, Miss Worlock,' said Jody. 'He won't get in your way. Suppose we say tomorrow afternoon for the concert? Then we can invite all the parents.'

'Tomorrow, dearie?' said Miss Worlock. 'That's a bit soon. You won't have time to learn the tunes, will you?'

'Oh, we'll practise very hard tonight, I promise we will,' said Jody. 'We ought to

be going home now. I'll put up posters
for the concert, and tell everyone about
it. We'll see you in the school hall at two
o'clock tomorrow for a practice, shall
we?'

'All right, dearie,' said Miss Worlock. 'I
must say, you're being very nice to
Wilhelmina today. I don't know what's
come over you all. See you tomorrow.
Cheeri-bye!' And off she went.

'What are you up to, Jody?' asked
Pete, when Miss Worlock had gone.

'There's no time to explain,' said Jody.
'I'm rushing off home to make some
posters. See you tomorrow.'

When Thomas and Pete came to school
next day, they saw the posters that Jody
had put up:

SCHOOL CONCERT
THIS AFTERNOON!
The St Barty's School Orchestra
will perform under the direction of
MISS WILHELMINA WORLOCK
At 2.30 p.m. Don't be late!

'I hope you know what you're doing, Jody,' said Pete.

'What I've got in mind is risky,' said Jody, 'but it might just work. Now, we need to carry the fish tank over to the hall. Come and help me.'

The fish tank was very heavy, but they managed to move it safely, and set it up behind the stage, where it was hidden by a curtain. Then they put out music stands for the concert.

At two o'clock, everyone who could play an instrument arrived in the school hall for a rehearsal. Hamish Bigmore was there, with his double bass. 'Why, if it isn't my star pupil,' said Miss Worlock, beaming at him. Hamish and Miss Worlock had always got on well. 'Now,' she called, 'we'll have another go at that piece we were playing last time, when stupid Majeika spoilt everything.' She raised her conductor's stick. 'One, two, three!'

The whole orchestra began playing the piece of music called 'The Elephant', which was a double bass solo for Hamish Bigmore. Like last time, Thomas and Pete had to do all the hard work on the double bass, fingering the right notes, while Hamish merely sawed away with the bow. And like last time, the noise was terrible.

'Stop!' screeched Miss Worlock. 'This won't do! My star pupil is playing

brilliantly, but the rest of you – you
deserve to be turned into toads. Try
again!'

They tried again. The noise was even
worse: screeching, groaning, scraping
and howling from all the instruments.
No one had done any practice at all.

'Right! I warned you!' screamed Miss
Worlock. 'Toads I said, and toads you

shall all be.' She muttered a spell, and the school hall grew dark. Thomas, Pete and Jody found themselves dropping to the floor and becoming smaller and smaller, while their skin grew scaly. In a moment, they were all hopping about the hall as toads – all except Hamish Bigmore.

'Wilhelmina wasn't going to turn her little star pupil into a toad,' Miss Worlock cooed at him. 'Oh no. She's going to go

off with him and start the School of Music somewhere else, and leave all this silly lot hopping about as toads for the rest of their silly lives. Come along, my star pupil.'

At this moment, the door of the school hall opened, and people began to come in. The first of the parents were arriving for the concert.

Miss Worlock stopped in her tracks. 'Er, good afternoon, ladies and gentlemen,' she called. 'Wilhelmina's concert has had to be cancelled, because all the children have gone away on a school trip, and they won't be back for days and days. But instead, Wilhelmina's star pupil, Hamish Bigmouth, will give a solo recital on the double bass. Off you go!' she hissed to Hamish.

'Bigmore,' muttered Hamish crossly. 'And I can't play this silly thing without my slaves to help me.'

'Get on with it,' snarled Miss Worlock, 'or you'll be a toad too.'

Hamish picked up the double bass and tried to play it by himself. The noise was awful. 'Very well!' screamed Miss Worlock. 'You're going to be a toad, too!'

'Help!' shouted Hamish. 'Listen, everyone, she's lying when she says

they've all gone on a school trip. She's turned them into toads. Stop her before she does it to me!'

The parents began to shout and scream, as they saw the mass of toads jumping about on the stage. One of the fathers stepped forward.

'I happen to be a Chief Inspector of Police,' he said, showing Miss Worlock his official card. 'I arrest you for witchcraft, and turning children into toads.' And he gripped Miss Worlock firmly by the shoulder. 'You'll probably get life imprisonment,' he warned her.

'All right, all right, dearie,' muttered Miss Worlock. 'It was just a silly mistake. Spell coming up.' She started to mutter, and the hall grew dark again. In a moment, Thomas, Pete and Jody found themselves back in their own shapes.

'Very well,' said the Chief Inspector.

'Don't try it again, madam, or it'll be prison for you.'

Miss Worlock gave a shriek and ran out of the door.

'Poor old Wilhelmina,' said a voice. Jody turned. It was Mr Majeika, stepping out on to the stage from where the fish tank stood. 'She doesn't have much luck, does she? But she's done the trick for me. Was that your idea, Jody?'

'Yes, Mr Majeika,' said Jody. 'I reckoned that if she turned us all into toads, as she probably would when she got cross, and then turned us back again, *you* might get turned back too. But it wouldn't have worked without Hamish Bigmore giving her away to the parents.'

'That's the funny thing about Hamish,' said Thomas. 'He's the school nuisance, but somehow he has the knack of making things come out right in the end.'

3.   A model pupil

Whenever it rained, water dripped through the roof of Class Three's classroom. The buildings at St Barty's School were rather old and worn out, but whenever Mr Majeika asked Mr Potter if the roof could be mended, he was told that there wasn't enough money.

However, one day Mr Potter told Mr Majeika that he had some good news. 'We've got enough money to deal with that leaking roof, Majeika.'

'That's wonderful, Mr Potter,' said Mr Majeika. 'Will you be able to get it mended soon?'

'Better than that,' said Mr Potter. 'You're going to have a completely new classroom. The people who look after

school buildings say that Class Three simply isn't safe. It's going to have to be pulled down and replaced with a brand new room.'

'Oh, I am glad,' said Mr Majeika. 'Can we get somebody clever to design a nice new classroom for us?'

Mr Potter frowned. 'There's not enough money to pay an architect or a designer,' he said. 'I think we'll have to choose one of the ready-made classrooms that the school-buildings people supply. Here, I'll show you some pictures of them.'

He opened a file, and showed Mr Majeika some very dreary pictures of dull-looking classrooms of different shapes and sizes.

'Oh dear,' said Mr Majeika. 'They don't look very nice.' Then he had an idea. 'Supposing,' he said to Mr Potter, 'that I held a competition among all the children in Class Three, and got them to do their own designs for the new classroom. If the winning design was really good, maybe we could get it built?'

Mr Potter scratched his head. 'It's a very unusual idea,' he said, 'but I don't see why we shouldn't try it. The children will have to work fast, though. We need a finished design in a week from now, so that the builders can start work.'

When Mr Majeika explained the idea to Class Three, everyone was excited – everyone, that is, except Hamish Bigmore.

'Who wants to design a classroom?' he groaned. 'Classrooms are boring. I'd rather design the biggest superstore in the world, or a bunker for secret missiles. Who wants to waste time with a silly classroom?'

Thomas, Pete and Jody, on the other hand, were very keen indeed. 'Can two or three of us work together?' Pete asked Mr Majeika.

'If you really want to,' said Mr Majeika. 'But the more entries for the competition the better.'

'Tell you what,' said Jody to Thomas and Pete, 'you two do a joint design together, and I'll do one by myself. I'm sure I can think of something.'

'I bet you ours'll be the best,' said
Thomas, though actually he hadn't got
the faintest notion what to put in his
ideal classroom. He was depending on
Pete.

'You can use the last lesson this
afternoon for beginning your designs,'
said Mr Majeika. 'And then as it's Friday,
you can finish them over the weekend.'

During the last lesson, they all got down to work, using large sheets of paper. Only Hamish Bigmore refused to do any drawing, and sat flicking paper pellets at the rest of Class Three. Mr Majeika tried to stop him, but since he'd turned himself into a lobster he was even more careful than usual not to lose his temper with Hamish. So in the end he left Hamish alone, and went round looking at the drawings.

They were rather disappointing. Most people had begun by drawing a big plan of the classroom as it was at present, and now they were filling in details like 'Mr Majeika's table' and 'Table for fish tank'. No one seemed to have any interesting ideas.

When the bell went for the end of afternoon school, Mr Majeika said: 'I haven't seen any likely winners yet. To tell you the truth, none of you has improved on the pictures of new classrooms that Mr Potter showed me.'

'Well, it's very hard, Mr Majeika,' said Thomas. 'We can't get any ideas. Have you got any good suggestions?'

Mr Majeika shook his head. 'It isn't supposed to be me making the suggestions,' he said. 'This is your competition. I know, maybe you'd get some better ideas if you tried making a model of the new classroom, rather than just doing a drawing. Why don't you try that over the weekend?'

On the way home, Thomas said: 'A model will be even harder than a drawing. I'm just no good at making models. And neither is Pete.'

'Oh, I don't know,' said Pete. 'I'll have a go. What about you, Jody?'

'I'm beginning to get a good idea,' said

Jody, smiling. 'See you on Monday morning.'

On Monday, lots of people in Class Three came into school carrying models made out of cardboard boxes, bits of yoghurt pots, and other things like that. Some of the models looked pretty useless – 'I don't think I fancy a classroom made out of old loo rolls,' said Thomas, looking at one boy's entry for the competition – but others were brightly painted and looked exciting.

During the morning, while everyone was finishing off homework, and reading books about the term's project, Mr Majeika went round inspecting the models. 'There are lots of very good ones,' he said to Class Three just before the lunch break. 'I'm going to find it very hard to choose a winner.'

'They're all rubbish,' shouted Hamish

Bigmore, who of course hadn't bothered
to make a model during the weekend.
'Chuck 'em in the dustbin.'

Jody put her hand up. 'I've got an
idea, Mr Majeika,' she said.

'Yes, Jody?' asked Mr Majeika. 'What
is it?'

'I'd rather tell you in private,' said
Jody. 'It's – well, it's rather a *magical*
idea.'

'Magical load of rubbish,' sneered Hamish Bigmore, barging past Jody on his way to lunch, even before the bell had gone.

'Well, Jody?' asked Mr Majeika, when everyone else had left the classroom.

'What I thought, Mr Majeika,' said Jody, 'was that the easiest way of judging which model is the best would be to – well, to *go into* them.'

'But you can't go into a model,' said Mr Majeika. 'It's too tiny.'

'You could make *us* tiny too,' said Jody. 'Or better still, you could make the models bigger, big enough for us to walk about in them.'

Mr Majeika thought for a few minutes. 'I'm not sure about making everyone smaller,' he said. 'It's one of those risky spells that might have dreadful results if it went at all wrong. But making the models bigger shouldn't be difficult, and I can't imagine that any harm would come of it. Let's try it after lunch.'

When Class Three were back in their places, Mr Majeika explained what was going to happen. 'I'm going to choose a shortlist of the three or four best models, and then I'm going to make each of them bigger – much bigger – so that we can walk about in them, and try them out, and see which really is the best of all.'

Everyone cheered when they heard this. Even Hamish Bigmore looked quite interested, and didn't make any rude remarks for once. 'Now,' said Mr Majeika, 'whose model shall we try first?'

Of course, at this, a forest of hands shot up, and everyone began yelling: 'Mine! Mine! My model is the best, Mr Majeika. Do try mine!'

By the time Mr Majeika had managed

to quieten them all down, Melanie was crying. 'Boo hoo! I know you're not going to choose my model, Mr Majeika. I never win anything. Boo hoo!'

Mr Majeika went over to Melanie's table, and peered at the model she had made. 'That's very good, Melanie,' he said. 'I don't think that everyone will like all the things you've put in your new classroom, but why don't we try it and see?'

Everyone groaned at this, except Jody, who said: 'It's only fair to let Melanie have a chance, if she's made a good model. Let's take it out into the playground, Mr Majeika, so that there will be plenty of room for it to grow.'

Melanie carried her model outside, and everyone followed. She put it down in the middle of the playground, and Mr Majeika waved his hands over it and muttered some words. The model began to grow. It grew, and grew, and grew, until it was standing as high as Class Three's old classroom.

There was a door in the side of it. Melanie opened it, and said: 'Come on, everyone, and see the pretty little classroom I've invented.'

They all followed her through the door. 'This doesn't look like a classroom at all,' said Thomas. 'It looks like a nursery.'

So it did. The walls were painted pink, with pretty little flowers stencilled on them, and the room was filled with soft toys. An enormous teddy bear stood in one corner, and there was even a play-pen. A poster on the wall showed you the letters of the alphabet in pretty colours.

'Strewth,' said Pete. 'So this is what

Melanie wants school to be like.'

Suddenly another door opened, and in stepped a woman in a dress patterned with pretty flowers. 'Hello, kiddie-winks,' she said. 'Have you come to see Aunty Jemima's Nursery? Isn't that nice? Come and sit on the floor, kiddie-winks, and I'll find a nice cuddly teddy for each of you, and then I'll read you all a story about a sweet little rabbit called Little Bluebell.'

'No you flaming well won't,' said Hamish Bigmore. 'I'm getting out of here.' He didn't even bother to go through the door, but elbowed his way through one of the walls, which was made of cardboard and gave way when he pushed.

This seemed to end the spell, because the model shrank to its small size again, leaving everyone standing in the playground. There was no sign of Aunty Jemima.

'Boo hoo!' howled Melanie. 'Hamish has spoilt my classroom.'

'I didn't know there was going to be a teacher in it, Mr Majeika,' said Thomas.

'Neither did I,' said Mr Majeika. 'I knew Melanie had made a toy figure of a teacher to go with her model, but I hadn't expected it to come alive.'

'We'd better make figures for our models too,' said Jody. 'It'll be much more fun if there are people in them.'

'All right,' said Mr Majeika, 'But you'll have to wait till tomorrow to go inside the next model. That's enough for this afternoon.'

The next day, Mr Majeika chose Thomas and Pete's model. They carried it out into the playground, and Mr Majeika made it grow bigger. Then everyone looked for the door.

'There isn't one,' said Pete. 'Leastways, not an ordinary door. You climb up this ladder and go in by the roof.'

He led the way. On the roof was a trapdoor, and when you went through it, you found yourself at the top of a long slide. 'Whee!' shouted Thomas, sliding

down it. 'Isn't this fun, Mr Majeika?'

'Yes,' said Mr Majeika doubtfully,
sliding down after him, 'but it doesn't
look much like a classroom.'

It certainly didn't. At the bottom of the
slide were roundabouts, roller-coasters,
and other exciting fairground rides.

For half an hour, Class Three had a
wonderful time trying out everything.

Even Hamish Bigmore seemed to be enjoying himself. Then, out of nowhere, a cross-looking man appeared. 'He's the figure we made,' whispered Thomas to Jody. 'He was meant to be a nice friendly teacher, but he didn't come out right.'

The man was big and rather lopsided and looked as if his head had been fastened on wrong. 'Oi, you lot!' he yelled. 'Oo said you could come in 'ere without paying? That's fifty pounds you owe me for using these rides without permission.'

'Don't pay any attention to him,' grunted Hamish Bigmore, and, just as he had with Melanie's model, he elbowed his way through the cardboard wall. Once again the model shrank, the man disappeared, and everyone was left standing in the playground.

'I said classroom, not fairground,'

smiled Mr Majeika at Thomas and Pete. 'That won't do at all. It's Jody's turn tomorrow – we'll see what she's come up with.'

When they carried Jody's model out into the playground next afternoon, and Mr Majeika made it bigger by magic, it looked very ordinary at first. A plain door had 'Class Three' written on it in neat writing, and when Jody opened the door and everyone followed her in, they were disappointed to find that the room looked just the same as their old classroom, except that everything was cleaner and newer.

'Boring!' said Hamish Bigmore, yawning. 'Stupid old Jody hasn't got any ideas.'

'Oh yes I have,' said Jody. 'The first lesson is French.'

A door at the back of the classroom

opened, and in stepped a French waiter,
carrying a large tray of delicious food.
'*Bonjour messieurs et mesdames*,' he said.
''Ello, ladies an' gentlemen. For your
French lesson today, 'ere is a delicious
French lunch.'

They all got down to the meal greedily.
There was lovely crusty French bread,
and delicious cheese and cold meats, and

everything had its name clearly written on it in French. 'I thought this would be a good way to do lessons,' Jody explained to Mr Majeika. 'Learning French from being served by a French waiter, and things like that.'

'It sounds a nice idea, Jody,' said Mr Majeika. 'But what are you going to do about maths?'

'You'll see,' said Jody, and called out 'Maths lesson!' in a loud voice.

The door opened, and in came a man in very old-fashioned clothes and a long wig. 'Greetings, gentle folk,' he said. 'My name is Sir Isaac Newton, and I was a very famous mathematician in my day, and this young lady here –' (he pointed at Jody) '– has invited me to come and teach you all.'

'I've had enough of this,' grumbled Hamish Bigmore, pushing his way out through the cardboard wall as usual.

'I call that a real pity,' said Thomas, as he watched the model shrink to its ordinary size. 'Jody's idea was very good.'

'Yes, wasn't it?' said Mr Majeika. 'It's certainly the best idea so far. But we've still got Hamish Bigmore's model to try out tomorrow. He's actually bothered to make one, so we ought to give him a chance.'

'I can imagine how horrid it'll be,' said Pete.

'Yes,' said Jody, 'but what sort of horrid? With Hamish, you never can tell.'

When Hamish carried his model out into the playground the next afternoon, everyone could see that it was made of little plastic sections. 'He's built it out of Lego,' said Thomas. 'What a cheat.'

When Mr Majeika had made the model grow bigger, Hamish led the way inside, and shut the door behind them. It was made of Lego inside too, though of course it was now giant Lego. All the tables and chairs and other things were brightly coloured plastic, with sharp edges.

'Here's the winner all right!' shouted Hamish. 'Isn't it smart?'

'Yes, Hamish,' said Mr Majeika, 'but what sort of lessons can you do in it?'

'That's just what I'm going to show you,' crowed Hamish. He pressed a button, and one of the pieces of giant Lego flew open, revealing a kind of chest or store cupboard. Inside were some enormous guns. 'The first lesson,' said Hamish, 'is how to fire a Death Ray Gun.' He took one of the guns, pointed it at a target on the wall, and pressed the

trigger. There was a flash of light and a nasty smoky smell, and the target melted.

'That looks dangerous,' whispered Jody. 'I think we ought to be getting out of here.'

Mr Majeika felt the same. 'Thank you, Hamish,' he said, 'but that's enough of guns. Let's get back to our real classroom, and decide who's going to be the winner.'

'I've decided that already,' said

Hamish, still holding the Death Ray Gun. 'My classroom is easily the best, so it's going to win, isn't it, Mr Majeika?' he asked, in a threatening voice. 'If it *doesn't* win, just think of all the nasty things I can do with this gun. It can melt anything plastic, so won't I have fun with everyone's lunch-boxes, not to mention the frames of your glasses, Mr Majeika!'

'So that's your game, is it, Hamish?' said Mr Majeika. 'Hamish! Hamish!'

Everyone wondered why Mr Majeika was calling Hamish's name like this. But then a door at the back of the classroom opened and in came *another* Hamish. He was made of Lego, and moved his plastic arms and legs and head very stiffly, but there was no doubt about it being Hamish.

'W-who are you?' stuttered the real

Hamish, looking at the plastic version of himself.

'I'm the Hamish Bigmore of the new classroom,' said the plastic Hamish. 'And you better give me back my Death Ray Gun, or else!'

'Shan't,' said the real Hamish, attempting to push the plastic Hamish out of the way. But the plastic Hamish was hard and strong, and it gave the real Hamish such a shove that he went reeling against the plastic walls of the

classroom. Though they were much stronger than the cardboard of other people's models, they gave way beneath the weight of Hamish, and the Lego classroom collapsed around everyone, and shrank at the same time, so that in a moment Class Three were standing in the playground in front of a small heap of bits of Lego.

'That was a near thing, Mr Majeika,' said Thomas, while the real Hamish picked himself up and muttered crossly. 'Was it your idea to put the plastic Hamish in the Lego classroom?'

Mr Majeika nodded. 'I guessed there'd be some trouble from Hamish if I didn't find someone who was a match for him. Jody, I think your idea ought to be the winner. We certainly don't want to have Hamish's model for our new classroom.'

'We don't,' laughed Jody. 'Though it's

nice to know that our Hamish isn't the worst trouble-maker you could imagine – that somewhere, there's another version of him who's *even worse!*'

Read more in Puffin

For complete information about books available from Puffin – and Penguin – and how to order them, contact us at the appropriate address below. Please note that for copyright reasons the selection of books varies from country to country.

www.puffin.co.uk

In the United Kingdom: Please write to Dept EP, Penguin Books Ltd,
Bath Road, Harmondsworth, West Drayton, Middlesex UB7 0DA

In the United States: Please write to Penguin Group (USA), Inc., P.O. Box 12289,
Dept B, Newark, New Jersey 07101–5289 or call 1–800–788–6262

In Canada: Please write to Penguin Books Canada Ltd,
10 Alcorn Avenue, Suite 300, Toronto, Ontario M4V 3B2

In Australia: Please write to Penguin Books Australia Ltd,
250 Camberwell Road, Camberwell, Victoria 3124

In New Zealand: Please write to Penguin Books (NZ) Ltd,
Private Bag 102902, North Shore Mail Centre, Auckland 10

In India: Please write to Penguin Books India Pvt Ltd,
11 Panscheel Shopping Centre, Panscheel Park, New Delhi 110 017

In the Netherlands: Please write to Penguin Books Netherlands bv,
Postbus 3507, NL–1001 AH Amsterdam

In Germany: Please write to Penguin Books Deutschland GmbH,
Metzlerstrasse 26, 60594 Frankfurt am Main

In Spain: Please write to Penguin Books S. A., Bravo Murillo 19,
1° B, 28015 Madrid

In Italy: Please write to Penguin Italia s.r.l.,
Via Felice Casati 20, I–20124 Milano

In France: Please write to Penguin France S. A.,
17 rue Lejeune, F–31000 Toulouse

In Japan: Please write to Penguin Books Japan, Ishikiribashi Building,
2–5–4, Suido, Bunkyo-ku, Tokyo 112

In South Africa: Please write to Longman Penguin Southern Africa (Pty) Ltd,
Private Bag X08, Bertsham 2013